For Suzanne

First published in Great Britain by HarperCollins Children's Books in 2007
First published in paperback in 2008
This edition published as part of a gift set in 2008

Text and illustrations copyright © Oliver Jeffers 2007

ISBN-13: 978-0-00-728885-4

1 3 5 7 9 10 8 6 4 2

Visit our website at: www.harpercollinschildrensbooks.co.uk

Printed in China

The Way Back Home

Oliver Jeffers

HarperCollins *Children's Books*

Once there was a boy,

and one day, as he was putting
his things back in the cupboard,
he found an aeroplane.

He didn't remember leaving it in there but
he thought he'd take it out for a go right away.

The plane lifted off the ground
and up into the sky...

higher   and higher   and higher.

Suddenly the plane spluttered...

phut

phut

phut

phut

it had run out of petrol.

Now the boy was stuck on the moon.
What was he to do?

He was all alone and afraid
and soon his torch began to go out.

Up in space someone
else was in trouble too.

His engine had
broken down...

and steering the ship
towards a flicker of light,
he landed on the moon
with a bump.

Both the boy and the Martian could hear noises in the dark and both feared the worst.

But as their eyes
got used to the dark,
they both realised
they'd met someone
else in trouble.

They weren't
alone any more.

The boy showed the Martian his
empty petrol tank and the Martian
showed the boy his broken engine.

Together they thought of ways to fix their machines and how to get them both back home.

The boy jumped down to earth to get the things they would need...

right
down
into
the
sea...

and swam towards home.

But by the time he got there, the boy was tired out so he sat in his favourite chair, just to catch his breath.

His favourite programme was just starting and he settled down to watch.

Suddenly he
remembered what he
should be doing and rushed
off to the cupboard to
get what he needed.
He ran outside and
shouted. But there was
no reply, he couldn't
be heard.

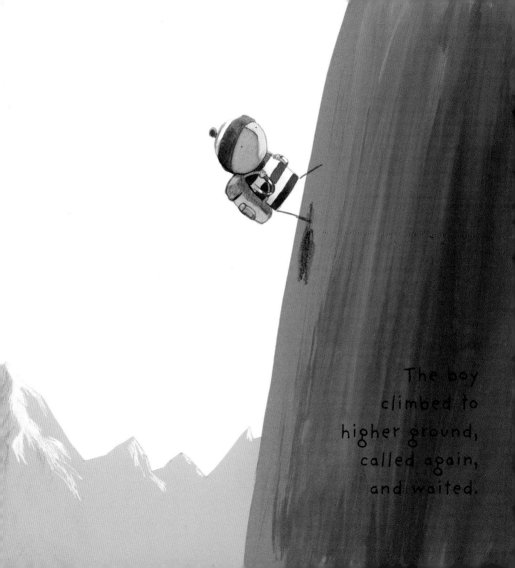

The boy
climbed to
higher ground,
called again,
and waited.

This time,
a rope
was lowered.

The boy
began to climb
and the Martian
began to pull,
and soon the
boy was back
on the moon.

The boy fixed up the Martian's engine
with the right spanner and the
Martian filled the boy's petrol tank.

They said goodbye and thanked
each other for their help.

They wondered if they'd
ever meet again.

After a long night
they were both finally
off the moon.

The boy went one way and the Martian went another, both on their way back home.

hello? hello? *